GO TO SLEEP, GROUNDHOG!

by JUDY COX

illustrated by PAUL MEISEL

Holiday House / New York

Text copyright © 2004 by Judy Cox
Illustrations copyright © 2004 by Paul Meisel
All Rights Reserved
Printed in the United States of America
The text type is Providence Sans.
The artwork was created with acrylic paints
and gouache on paper.
www.holidayhouse.com
First Edition

Library of Congress Cataloging-in-Publication Data
Cox, Judy
Go to sleep, Groundhog! / by Judy Cox ; illustrated by Paul Meisel.— 1st ed.
p. cm.
Summary: When Groundhog is unable to sleep,
he experiences autumn and winter holidays he never knew about,
and then he finally falls asleep before Groundhog Day.
ISBN 0-8234-1645-3 (hardcover)
[1. Woodchuck—Fiction. 2. Groundhog Day—Fiction.
3. Holidays—Fiction.] I. Meisel, Paul, ill. II.Title.
PZ7.C83835 Go 2003
[E]—dc21   2002024124

Groundhog went to bed on Columbus Day, just like he always did. He brushed his teeth.

He put on his jammies.

He set his clock for February 2. Then he curled
up in his warm cozy bed.

He closed his eyes. He tossed and turned, but
he couldn't get to sleep. Finally, he got out of bed.
He peered at his clock. Half-past October.

Groundhog poked his nose outside his burrow.
The moon was full.

"I'll just go for a little walk," he said. "Maybe
that will make me sleepy."

Groundhog went outside. He saw things he'd never seen before! Raggedy scarecrows and grinning jack-o'-lanterns. Children dressed up like pirates, cowboys, and princesses.

Halloween Witch flew down.

"What are *you* doing up?" she said. "It's almost winter. You should be in bed!"

Witch flew Groundhog home on her broomstick. She tucked him in. She read him a ghost story.

She gave him a glass of apple cider.

Groundhog curled up in his warm cozy bed. He closed his eyes. He tossed and turned, but he couldn't get to sleep. Finally, he got out of bed. He peered at his clock. Half-past November.

He poked his nose outside his burrow. The leaves were red and yellow.

"I'll just go for a little walk," he said. "Maybe that will make me sleepy."

Groundhog went outside. He saw things he'd never seen before! Tall yellow corn shocks and round orange pumpkins. Turkeys gobbling in the barnyard.

"What are *you* doing up?" Turkey said. "It's almost winter. You should be in bed, and I should be making myself scarce."

Turkey took Groundhog home. He tucked him in. He read him a story about Pilgrims. He gave him a slice of pumpkin pie.

Groundhog curled up in his warm cozy bed. He closed his eyes. He tossed and he turned, but he couldn't get to sleep. Finally, he got out of bed. He peered at his clock. Half-past December.

Groundhog poked his nose outside his burrow.
Stars twinkled overhead.

"I'll just go for a little walk," he said. "Maybe
that will make me sleepy."

Groundhog went outside. He saw things he'd
never seen before! Colored lights glowing on
some houses, candles shining in windows, holly
wreaths hanging on doors. He heard sleigh bells
chiming in the air.

Santa flew down in his sleigh. "What are *you* doing up?" Santa said. "It's winter. You should be in bed!"

Santa took Groundhog home in his sleigh. He tucked him in. He read him a Christmas story. He gave him a glass of milk and a cookie.

Groundhog curled up in his warm cozy bed. He closed his eyes. He didn't toss and he didn't turn. And soon he fell asleep.

"BRRRRINGGGG!"

Groundhog opened one eye. "It can't be time to get up yet," he grumbled. "I just got to sleep!"

"BRRRRINGGGG!"

He peered at his clock. February 2.

Groundhog yawned and stretched. He tumbled
out of his burrow. Snow glittered on the ground.
The sun was out. The sky was blue.

Groundhog saw his shadow. "What am I doing up?" he said. "There are six more weeks of winter coming! I should be in bed!"

He hurried back inside. He ate a bedtime snack. He read himself a bedtime story. Then he tucked himself into his warm cozy bed.

And he pulled up the covers, closed his eyes, and went to sleep.

ABOUT GROUNDHOG DAY

Groundhog Day is celebrated on February 2. According to tradition, on this day the groundhog wakes from winter hibernation. He leaves his underground den and peers outside. If the day is sunny, the groundhog sees his shadow and becomes frightened. He scurries back into his burrow, and we have six more weeks of winter. If the weather is cloudy and the groundhog does not see his shadow, he stays outside and spring begins.

In the days before weather satellites and television, it was hard for farmers to know when the harsh winter was over so they could plant crops.

There are many superstitions involving predicting the weather by animal behavior. In Europe, badgers, hedgehogs, and bears were used to forecast the coming of spring. When German settlers arrived in North America, they used the small furry groundhog (also known as a woodchuck) because it wakes from hibernation in February and is easily observed in the eastern United States and Canada.

Groundhogs are rodents that belong to the marmot family. They live in underground burrows and hibernate in them from October to February. Their diet consists of tender green plants. They cannot really predict the weather.